WAIT WATCH & LOVE

Lovingly Hand Crafted by MOMMA BEE

Dedicated to my Lily,
A true inspiration of how to love

Lily walked into her garden.

"What will I find today?" she wondered.

Sometimes Lily would find seeds and plant them.

Sometimes the seeds would float in on the BREEZE...

... and just start growing.

First there would be a **FLASH** of GREEN

and then
a
struggle
to
the
sun.

more
water,

And the flowers grew and grew and GREW.

As Lily poked among the flowerbeds this morning, to her

DELIGHT,

she saw a plant growing that she had never seen before.

Just then Miss Tulip
poked her EXPERT nose
over her TRIM fence and said,

"OH, LILY!

Watch out for that one!!
It's a WEED.
Don't let that into your garden
or you'll regret it!"

Lily STOPPED.

"What's a WEED?"

The question seemed TOO BIG for one little girl to answer...

...so she asked her mother.

Her mom took Lily in her arms and answered thoughtfully.

"Well, Lily... I guess a weed is a plant
you don't want to have in your garden."

Lily let that idea **GROW** as she watched the tender new plant push its way to the light.

DEFINITELY NOT A WEED —

When it blossomed, Lily smiled.

Word traveled far and wide about Lily's
GARDEN.
It seemed she could grow just about everything with her
waiting and watching and loving.

And people CAME.

Some people
Lily
invited,

and
some people
just wandered in
on their
own.

And they stayed.

Lily would WAIT...

...and WATCH and LOVE every one of them.

Lily found that
she could just tell if people needed more SUNSHINE.

more water,

Or just more space.

And the people healed.

One day
a strange boy
wandered into Lily's
garden and sat
wearily on
a bench.

Lily STOPPED.

"What's a BAD SEED?"

The question seemed TOO BIG for one little girl to answer...

...so she asked her mother.

Her mom took Lily in her arms and answered thoughtfully.

"Well, Lily... I guess a 'bad seed' is a person you don't want to have in your life."

Lily let that idea grow as she

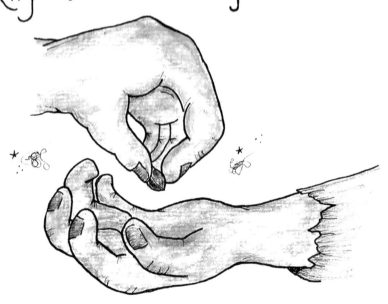

WAITED;

WATCHED,

and LOVED.

As Lily watched
her new friend blossom
she smiled.

· * ✿❀ * ·

" Definitely not a
bad seed, "
she whispered
to her flowers.

And they all agreed.

Hello from the Singing Bees!
All gather near.
Our family has stories you simply must hear.
We're rowdy and crazy and all kinds of fun.
And all of us so very different-- each one!

From Tova to baby with many between,
They'll show you adventures that you've only dreamed.
And e'en in the more common stories you'll find
Lessons that gently unfold to the mind.

Some of these kids will use magic, tis true...
And maybe you'll see there is magic in you!
For each one of our lives is a story to tell...
With so much to learn, if we'd just listen well.

So get yourself comfortably settled and then
Just open this book and the fun will begin.
My children will teach:
make you laugh, make you cry.
It's all up to you.  Come on, give it a try!

And maybe as you turn that last page you will see
A story to tell lies in you and in me!

Made in United States
Troutdale, OR
12/04/2024

25874906R00024